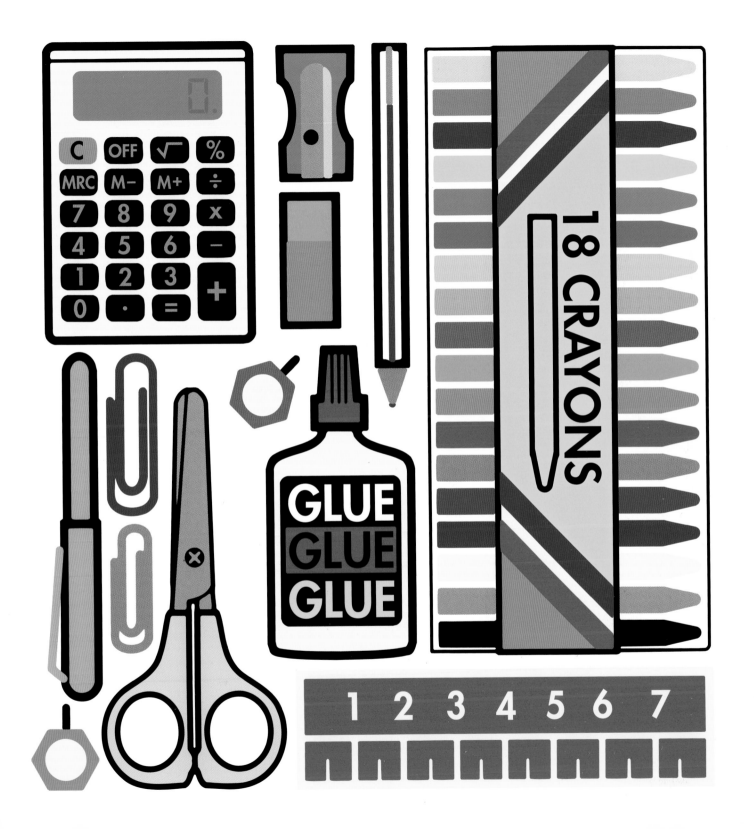

Published by
PEACHTREE PUBLISHING COMPANY INC.
1700 Chattahoochee Avenue
Atlanta, Georgia 30318-2112
www.peachtree-online.com

First published in Great Britain in 2018 by Jonathan Cape, an imprint of Penguin Random House Children's
First United States version published in 2018 by Peachtree Publishers
First United States trade paperback edition published in 2018 by Peachtree Publishers

The illustrations were rendered digitally.

Printed in May 2021 by Leo Paper in China
10 9 8 7 6 5 4 3 2 1 (hardcover)
10 9 8 7 6 5 4 3 2 (trade paperback)

HC: 978-1-68263-070-9
PB: 978-1-68263-058-7

Library of Congress Cataloging-in-Publication Data

Names: Bee, William, author, illustrator.
Title: Stanley's school / William Bee.
Description: First edition. | Atlanta : Peachtree Publishers, 2018. | "First published in Great Britain in 2018
by Jonathan Cape, an imprint of Penguin Random House Children's"—Title page verso. | Summary: It is
another busy day at school as Stanley and Hattie ready Little Woo, Sophie, and Benjamin for story time,
playtime, gardening, lunch, and nap time.
Identifiers: LCCN 2017056828 | ISBN 9781682630709
Subjects: | CYAC: Schools—Fiction. | Hamsters—Fiction. | Rodents—Fiction.
Classification: LCC PZ7.B38197 Svl 2018 | DDC [E]—dc23 LC record available at
https://lccn.loc.gov/2017056828

SCHOOL BUS

williambee
Stanley's
School

PEACHTREE
ATLANTA

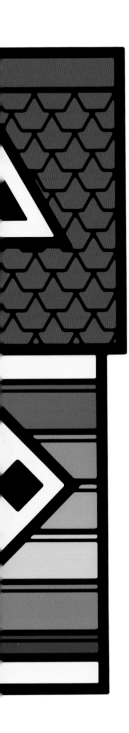

It's going to be another busy day at Stanley's School.

Hattie rings the bell. Ding, ding, ding.
Time for school!

The children hang up their hats,
bags, and teddy bears.

Stanley calls the children's names:
Little Woo, Sophie, and Benjamin.
All here!

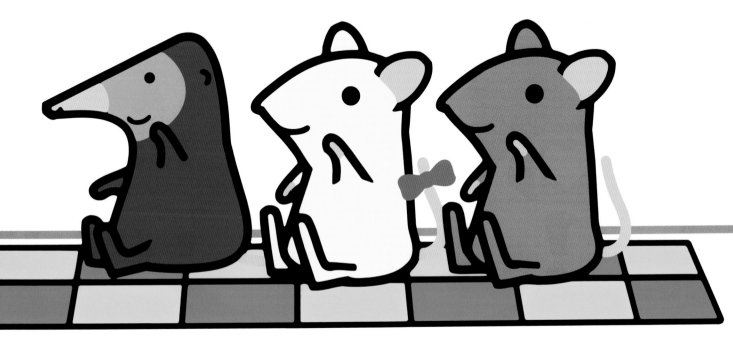

Stanley reads the children a story
about a dragon, a knight,
and a princess.

Sophie dresses up as the dragon,
Little Woo dresses up as a knight,
and Benjamin dresses up as the princess.

After storytime—it's playtime! Little Woo, Sophie, and Benjamin act out the story Stanley has just read to them.

But Benjamin has made up a new ending . . .
RAWRRR!

Stanley, Little Woo, Sophie, and Benjamin are all in the school's garden. They have come to measure their sunflowers.

Benjamin and Sophie have watered their sunflowers every day—don't they look big? But Little Woo forgot to water his.

After all that storytelling, measuring, and chasing about—it's time for lunch!

There is cheese and tomato pie for everyone!
Stanley has made some lemonade,
and Hattie has made a lovely fruit salad.

Then it's time
for a little nap.

Little Woo, Sophie, and Benjamin love painting!
Some of the paint ends up on the paper . . .

and the rest ends up on the floor,
the tables, and on Stanley and Hattie.

Hattie rings the bell. Ding, ding, ding.
It's time to go home!

Thank you, Stanley!
Thank you, Hattie!

Well! What a busy day!

Stanley's
House

by little woo

Time for supper!
Time for a bath!

And time for bed!
Goodnight, Stanley.

Stanley

If you liked **Stanley's School** then you'll love these other books about Stanley:

Stanley the Builder
HC: $14.95 / 978-1-56145-801-1

Stanley's Diner
HC: $14.95 / 978-1-56145-802-8

Stanley the Farmer
HC: $14.95 / 978-1-56145-803-5

Stanley's Garage
HC: $14.95 / 978-1-56145-804-2

Stanley the Mailman
HC: $14.95 / 978-1-56145-867-7

Stanley's Store
HC: $14.95 / 978-1-56145-868-4